Ben Stilliker

The Tale Of Willy Willys

DEDICATION

I hope you enjoy reading *The Tale of Willy Willys* as much as I enjoyed writing it. The *Tale* is based on what is credibly reported to be a true episode in the history of a 1926 Willys Overland.

Taking *The Tale of Willy Willys* from text to finished book was a pleasure because of the help of many old friends, as well as new friends I met during the process. I can't adequately thank them all but I'd like to give special thanks to my sister-in-law, Carol Porter. Most of all, I want to thank my friend since high school, Ron Elz, also known on the radio for decades as the personality he created, Johnny Rabbit. Ron (Johnny), a published author, was tireless in introducing me to the best artists, proof readers, book designers and publishers. This book is dedicated to Ron and my dear wife, June.

—Ben Hilliker

Artwork by Robert Shay

First Edition 2013
Released in conjunction with Mound City Publishing
2001 S. Hanley Rd., Suite 300, St. Louis MO 63144
314-781-0001

© Copyright 2013 by Ben Hilliker

ISBN 978-0-615-76351-4

Book designed by Cathy Wood

Printed in the United States of America

All rights reserved. This book may not be reproduced, in whole or in part, in any form (beyond that copying permitted by Section 107 and 108 of the U. S. Copyright Law and by reviewers or reporters for the public press), without written permission from the copyright holder.

Ben Hilliker

The Tale of Willy Willys

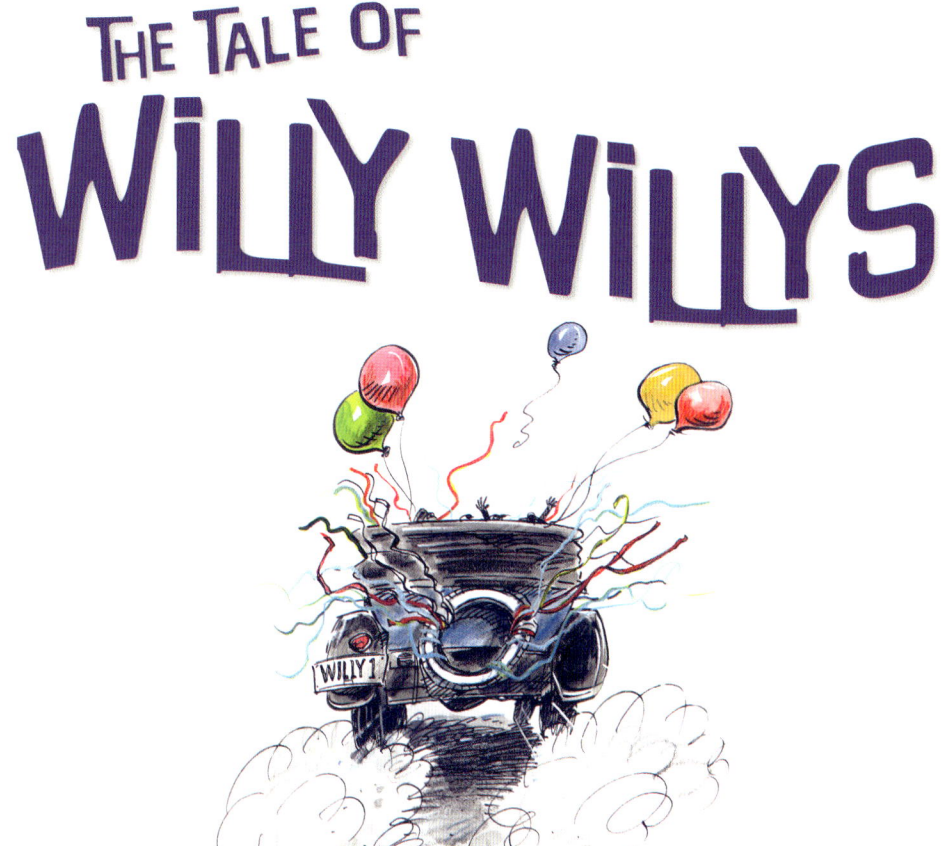

On a sunny, summer day, old Mr. and Mrs. Willys drove their car happily along a rolling, rocky, rural road. Bright sunlight shone on the green grass of the pastures, the fields of corn and the leafy trees of all sizes, while birds sat on the phone wires, swaying in the breeze and basking in the sun.

"What a wonderful, winding byway, Martha," said Mr. Willys. "We ought to drive along here more often, not just on our anniversary."

Mrs. Willys nodded and said, "That's true, Charlie," as they rolled past a white frame farmhouse that sat in the shade of big trees with long, leafy limbs.

Just then a man in blue bib overalls stepped into the road, in front of Mr. and Mrs. Willys, holding one hand high, hailing them to halt. Beyond the man, a truck, a big red farm truck, was backing off the road, toward a big, brown batch of brambles, briars and bushes.

"Howdy," said the man in overalls, when Mr. and Mrs. Willys stopped. "Our truck will be out of your way in a minute. We're just backing in to pick up the old Willys."

"Well!" exclaimed Mr. Willys, "*We're* the Willys and we may be old, but we don't need to be picked up. We don't need to be set down, put aside or turned around, carried, ferried or towed!"

"Oh, I see," chuckled the man, his thumbs in the straps of his bib overalls. "What a crazy, colossal coincidence. The Willys we're going to pick up is the old car over there," as he nodded toward a big, brown bunch of brambles, briars and bushes. "We're going to haul the Willys in for scrap. We won't get much for it, but then, at least, we'll be able to get that bothersome bunch of bushes, briars and brambles it's sitting in out of our pasture."

Mr. and Mrs. Willys turned and looked at the only brown place in a green pasture. There, sticking up through a twisted tangle of bushes', briars' and brambles' brown branches was the windshield of an old car. "Oh, Charlie," said Mrs. Willys, as she nudged him, "That old car has the same name as us. Let's go over and see it." Mr. Willys was already opening his door.

The man in overalls helped them into the field's tall grass, and together, Mr. and Mrs. Willys walked through the pasture to the twisted, twining tangle, through which the man who had been in the truck was already cutting a swath. As he continued to cut the briars, brambles, and bushes, more and more of the old Willys came into view. Mr. and Mrs. Willys could soon see it was a four-door, open-top car. Its wood-spoke wheels had sunk into the messy, mucky mud so far that the bottom of the Willys' body was down on the ground.

The car was rusty, crusty and dusty, with only a few flakes of blue paint left on the body and spokes. Black paint shared its fenders with rust. Mice had chewed holes in the back seat, while rusty springs were all that were left of the front seat. A few shreds of dirty canvas were the last remaining pieces of the top. One headlight was missing and the glass in the remaining headlight was broken. Mr. and Mrs. Willys put their arms around each other and looked at the Willys as if they were looking at a member of their family who was quite ill.

"Well," said the man from the truck, "Willy has seen better days."

"Willy?" asked Mr. Willys.

"Yep," said the man, "that's what folks used to call him. They called him Willy Willys. Mom and Dad have told us of how Grandma and Grandpa used to take Dad, Uncle Fred and Aunt Tilly, when they were children, everywhere in Willy. My gosh, they had great times with Grandma and Grandpa in the front seat, the children in the back seat and the top down. Willy rolled over the roads and took them to town to visit friends and he took them to royally rollicking, reveling, riverside picnics. Their picnic basket would be sitting on that running board you now see down in the mud. Willys' body and spokes were bright blue then. "Bluebird blue," they called it, and his fenders were gleaming black. Coming back from town, the kids would have big, bulbous, brightly colored balloons from the dime store and they'd watch them bobble and blow in the breeze, as Willy whistled along."

"That's right," said the man in blue overalls. "But Willy was there in winter too, with his top up and wind screens in place, a trusty, tried and true friend, keeping the cold wind off everyone.

It was during a snowstorm one night that Aunt Tilly, who was then only six, fell and broke her arm. Willy had been outside in the cold and was covered with snow, but started right up. Grandma sat on that back seat you now see full of mouse holes, holding young Aunt Tilly on her lap, while Grandpa drove. Willy took them through the freezing wind and the relentlessly swirling snow, over ice and through deep drifts of snow, to the warmth and care at the doctor's office."

By now, Mrs. Willys had pushed through the brambles, to the side of Willy, ignoring the thorns that caught on her dress. Rubbing her hands along the top of the window sills, not minding the dirt on them, she asked, in almost a whisper, "Charlie, what can we do for a deserted, distressed derelict that's dependably and diligently done its duty and shares our family name?"

Mr. Willys laughed. "Well, Martha, I've had a hard time thinking of something different to give you for our anniversary and I guess this could be something for me, too." Turning to the two men, he said, "Tell you what, fellows, I'll pay you the scrap value of poor old, worn-down Willy, if you'll haul him to my house instead of the scrap yard. I don't know what I'll do with him, though. No, I don't know."

The man with the big red truck and the man in blue overalls were happy. They hadn't really wanted to scrap Willy. They didn't know what would happen to Willy now, but maybe it would be something good.

The two men dug dirt away from in front of Willy so they could hook a chain to Willy's front axle. Then, with a winch on the front of the truck's bed, they began to pull on the chain, and the chain pulled on Willy. But Willy's wheels remained stuck down in the messy, muddy, mucky mire. The chain pulled harder and harder. "Oh, no," gasped Mrs. Willys, "something is going to break."

"Wait!" said Mr. Willys, "I think Willy's starting to move. Watch. His wheels are starting to turn."

And sure enough, Willy's wooden spoked wheels tenuously turned and climbed from the clutches of their earthen pits, as his rusty running boards began to rise from the ground. As the chain slowly pulled Willy onto the open bed of the truck, twisted, twining, tangled brown briars and brambles tugged tenaciously on all parts of Willy, trying to hold him back. When Willy finally sat on the back of the truck, some briars and brambles still clung to him. But Willy was free.

What a happy group rolled into town. The two men in the truck with Willy on the back smiled big smiles because they knew they weren't taking Willy to the scrap yard. Mr. and Mrs. Willys, following behind, felt years younger. To them it seemed almost as if they had a new member of their family. They didn't know what they were going to do with Willy, but they felt they were starting on a new adventure. Up on the bed of the truck, the wind whistled past Willy's hood and around his wheels as it had years ago. Something seemed to stir groggily within Willy, like someone waking from a long, long sleep.

"Am I awake for goodness sake, or am I dreaming, am I dreaming?"

Just then, the truck hit a big, bodacious, boulder of a bump, bouncing Willy like a rider on a bucking brahma bull.

"Ooooh," thought Willy, *"I surely felt that!"*

"Am I awake, for goodness sake,
or am I dreaming, am I dreaming?
No, I do feel air rushing by,
I'm on a truck bed, way up high,
my wheels are still, my motor's still,
yet I'm flying past field and hill.
Up on this truck bed, way up high,
I again, feel fresh air rushing by.
As I once did."

It was almost dusk when Willy was rolled off the truck bed and under the roof of the carport behind Mr. and Mrs. Willys' house. Willowy white wisteria wound up each post of the carport. It grew from ground to roof. Willy thought, "Oh, my goodness. A roof to keep rain off of me."

Mr. and Mrs. Willys stood with their arms around each other, looking at Willy, and Mrs. Willys whispered, "Charlie, it's getting late, but early tomorrow, let's wash and clean the mud, dirt and cobwebs off our Willy."

"Yes," said Mr. Willys, "and some fellows I know, can tell us who can do the giant, jumbo job of fixing Willy up."

As Mr. and Mrs. Willys walked into their house, a bit of moisture ran through the broken glass of Willy's one headlight and Willy thought, **"Somebody cares about me."**

Mr. Willys wasted no time, for in only a few days Willy found himself just within the drive-in door of Roscoe Rench's Restoration Shop. Roscoe Rench had a round, rosy-red face and wore a bright yellow shirt, dark blue pants and a look of happy excitement.

"Wow, wow, wow," he said as he walked around and around Willy. "I haven't seen a Willys Overland for a long time, and this one looks very solid for a car that's been outside for years."

"What's needed to fix Willy up?" asked Mr. Willys.

"Money," replied Roscoe Rench.

"Oh!" sighed Mr. Willys.

After a pause Roscoe Rench said, "Well, Willy is musty and crusty, he's rusted and busted, but I can make him just like new, I only need the word from you."

Mr. Willys and Mr. Rench walked into Mr. Rench's office, and for a long time Willy could hear them talking and sometimes laughing. Finally, they came out and walked over to Willy. Mr. Willys patted Willy on his rusty, crusty hood and then with a wave to Mr. Rench and one look back at Willy, walked out the door.

Mr. Rench called to his helper, Peter Putty. Together, Roscoe Rench and Peter Putty pushed Willy Willys across the floor of the shop—with Willy's flat tires going *scrunch*, *scrunch*, *scrunch*—and into a row of parked, old cars. Some of the cars were bright and shiny, and some more tired, torn and tattered than Willy.

No sooner was Willy in place than Roscoe's calico cat, Callie, rose from where she'd been napping, next to the soda machine, and sauntered over to Willy. With great poise, she leapt onto his running board and rubbed her back against Willy's doors. With a purr, she settled down on Willy's running board and resumed her nap.

The next few weeks were exciting for Willy.

Light through big windows and lights on the high ceiling of Roscoe's shop made it a cheery place. The light also showed it had been a while since the floor had been painted gray and the walls painted light yellow in some places, light green in others. A window box hung outside the window nearest Willy, and purple petunias peered through the pane.

All the cars welcomed Willy with voices only cars could hear. There was Reo Rita, the red, rumble seat, Reo roadster; Stuart Studebaker, the dark tan, doctor's coupe; beautiful Beulah Buick, a baby blue Riviera; and Martin, the maroon Mercury sedan. All the other cars welcomed Willy—all except the huge black Packard limousine, which ignored Willy.

When Willy asked his name, the Packard said, "Little fellow, to you, my name is, 'Sir.'" But Willy thought he heard a chuckle. "I have twelve cylinders and twenty-six coats of hand-rubbed paint," the Packard went on. "I wouldn't be associating with this pack of cars and you, if I didn't have a strep, carburetor throat."

Willy didn't know what a strep, carburetor throat was, but said, "Well, that must be a majestically magnificent malady, if you have it, Sir."

"Harumpf," said the Packard, but Willy thought he heard that chuckle again.

Willy was hellaciously, head-over-heels happy. After all the lonesome years under snow, rain and ice, tangled in twisting, twining briars, brambles and bushes, he was at peace, with a roof over his head and in felicitous friend's fellowship.

The next day, Roscoe Rench and his helpers walked around and around Willy, writing notes on clipboards. There was Roscoe's assistant mechanic, Buster Nuckles, in his white coveralls, with "Buster" stitched in red, on the front. There was the body repair man, Peter Putty, and his assistant, Sandy Rust, who wore a white T-shirt and tan work pants

covered with splotches of paint of every color in the world, it seemed. Around and around they went and crawled underneath, making notes on what needed to be fixed and what parts were needed. Willy began to woefully worry, as the lists got longer and longer.

"Oh," he moaned, "they're going to decide it's too much work to fix me up. They're going to scrap me and turn me into tin ash trays."

"No, No," chirped Reo Rita;
"Now don't get weepy and worried Willy,
when you fret you're being silly.
When I got here I was a mess
and worried too, I must confess.
But now you see, I'm bright and shining,
so don't be scared and feel like whining."

17

"Oh, I've seen some terrible cases," Stuart, the doctors coupe broke in, "They came here in critical condition, and rolled out the door as glamorous, eye-popping, show-stopping examples of exuberant energy."

All the cars pitched in to cheer Willy up. And it was good that they were there to encourage him, because soon, Buster Nuckles and Sandy Rust were taking Willy all apart. Each piece of Willy had to be cleaned, straightened, repaired and restored, or rejected and replaced. Under Willy's rear seat, Buster found an old string with a piece of yellow balloon tied to it, a green yo-yo and an old American flag with only forty-eight stars.

Willy would keep his courage up, but sometimes he'd start to think,
"Oh, I'm all in pieces.
I'm without wheels and up on jacks,
with my parts in crates and sacks;
I haven't my hood or a single door,
my motor and seats are on the floor."

Whenever he saw Willy worried, Martin Mercury would say,
"Cheer up Willy. You'll see a new day.
I was once all apart, like you,
but now you can see, I'm just like new.
My parts were in bins, in cans and pans,
 but now,
I'm the handsomest of sedans."

Martin thought it was all right to boast, if it cheered someone up.

"**Well,**" said Willy, "If I ever do get back together again, I don't think I'll be just like new. Mr. Willys can only spend so much. But I'm not complaining. For the first time in years, someone cares about me. I just hope they remember where they put all my parts and how they go together."

With encouragement from his friends, Willy's spirits rose skyward day after day, as he watched Buster work on his wheels and Roscoe work on his motor. He felt so clean after Sandy sanded all the rust off his body and fenders. Willy admired the way Peter patiently patched the worst places, cutting away bad spots and welding in fresh new metal. How it tickled when Peter sprayed Willy with shiny new bluebird blue and gleaming black paint.

One sunny morning, Willy could feel an excitement in the shop. His wheels were back on, with their new, wide whitewall tires and each wooden spoke painted shiny, bright, bluebird blue. Every one of his pieces was in place, clean and glowing. As Buster was connecting wires to Willy's spark plugs, Mr. and Mrs. Willys walked in the door.

"Well, well, welcome, Willys," said Roscoe. "We asked you to visit, because we're about to start Willy for the first time."

With that, Buster connected a battery to Willy's new wires, and Willy felt a tingle of electricity he'd not felt in years. Roscoe poured gas into the top of Willy's vacuum tank and then sat on the new black leatherette driver's seat. He pulled out Willy's choke and held the big, wood steering wheel. But, as his foot pushed the starter button on the floor, and Willy's motor turned over and over, Willy couldn't start. Everyone was watching and Willy shivered with embarrassment. Peter Putty, Sandy Rust and even Callie the cat had come over to watch.

"Oh, I'm trying so hard to start," groaned Willy to himself. *"I'm disappointing everyone and I'm so thirsty. Yes, I'm very thirsty."*

"It looks like we forgot this," said Buster as he reached under Willy's hood and opened the gas valve between Willy's vacuum tank and his motor.

"Oops," said Roscoe, his round, rosy-red face turning even redder. Roscoe pushed Willy's starter button again, and in a moment Willy's thirst was quenched as gas flowed through the open valve and into his motor. In another moment there was a **"pop!"**, then a **"pop! pop!"** followed by a **"Pop! Pop! Pop!"**, then **"Pop! Pop! Pop! Pop! purrerr-r-r-r"** and Willy's motor was running. Willy swelled with joy as everyone let out gleeful howls and cheers for him.

Roscoe pushed in Willy's clutch, shifted to low gear and as he let out the clutch, Willy moved himself forward. *"I'm moving, I'm moving, I'm moving!"* exclaimed Willy. *"No one's pushing or pulling me. I'm doing it all by myself again!"*

For the next two days, Roscoe and Buster double checked and adjusted all of Willy's parts.

On the third day, early in the morning, Mr. and Mrs. Willys were back again, this time with their two grandchildren and two of their grandchildren's friends. All of the other cars, knowing Willy was about to leave, congratulated Willy on looking so wonderful, and wished him well. Reo Rita said she hoped she'd see him at a car show. Martin Mercury said maybe he'd see Willy at a picnic or parade. Meanwhile, Mrs. Willys and the children tied red, white and blue streamers to Willy. Mr. Willys tied the flag Buster had found, to the top of Willy's windshield frame.

"Oh, you look sparkling, shiny and festive," called Greta, a gritty, grimy, gray Graham sedan that had arrived the week before, for Roscoe's restoration. **"I can hardly wait until they make me look new like you."**

Mr. and Mrs. Willys and the children climbed into Willy. Mrs. Willy called to Roscoe, Buster, Peter and Sandy, "Thanks to you, Willy and all of us have a lot of happy times ahead." The grandchildren and their friends held balloon strings as the balloons tugged on the strings, trying to fly. Mr. Willys pushed Willy's starter button and Willy's motor started, with a **"Pop!, Pop!, purrerr-r-r-r"**.

RRRRRRR

Mr. Willy paused just long enough to enjoy the sound of Willy's motor before calling out, "Hold on, kids," and letting out Willy's clutch.

Everyone cheered and laughed, as Willy moved forward. Willy rolled out of Roscoe's shop and onto the welcoming, sunny street, with red, white and blue streamers streaming, the old flag flying and balloons buoyantly bobbing.

"Charlie," said Mrs. Willys, "Willy is really himself again."

"Yes. And don't **we** feel younger again," exalted Mr. Willys.

As Willy picked up speed, he was beside himself with joy and sang,

> "I'll take you here,
> I'll take you there,
> I'll take you everywhere,
> because you care.
>
> Because you care,
> I feel fresh air,
> and I declare,
> I'll take you everywhere,
>   everywhere, everywhere."

Willy still delights in taking people for rides. If you should happen to see a blue Willys Overland with black fenders, filled with happy people, you just might be seeing Willy Willys and his friends, enjoying another deliciously delightful drive. After many drives, Peter Putty's paint is no longer quite as shiny. But the joy Willy brings to his riders shines as brightly as the day he left Roscoe Rench's Restoration Shop.

Glossary, Body Styles

1. **Rumble Seat Roadster**: A roadster is an open top car like today's convertibles but there is no back seat and the top does **not** go up and down with the push of a button. The top has to be put up and taken down by hand. There are no roll-up windows. Instead, in bad weather, transparent Isinglass "windscreens" are fastened to the tops of the doors. In good weather, the windscreens are usually stored under the seat. Once, many roadsters had a rumble seat. A rumble seat accommodates two people and is where a car's trunk would usually be. Riders would climb on a step on the back bumper and a step on the back fender to get in the rumble seat.

2. **Touring Car**: A touring car is an open top car with both front and rear seats. The top does not go up and down with the push of a button, but is put up and folded down by hand. As with a roadster, it has windscreens, not roll-up windows. A touring car almost always has four doors although a few have only two doors.

3. **Sedan**: A sedan is a car with a top that doesn't go down and with both front and back seats. Its passenger compartment is bigger than a coupe's. If it has a luggage compartment behind the back seat, it cannot be reached from the passenger compartment as with an SUV. Rather, the luggage compartment is called a "trunk" and is loaded and unloaded while standing behind the car. Nearly all sedans today have four doors but years ago many sedans had just two doors and the front seats folded forward to let people get to the back seat.

4. **Limousine**: A limousine is a car designed to be driven by a chauffeur. It is like a four door sedan but longer. There is usually a roll-up window in the back of the front seat so people sitting in the back can talk without the chauffeur hearing. It often has extra seats in the back.

5. **Doctors Coupe**: A coupe is a car with a top that doesn't go down and a smaller passenger compartment than a sedan, and has only two doors. Often there is no back seat. Coupes that had no back seat and were a dark color were often called doctors coupes because they were popular with doctors. The passenger compartment had just enough room for the doctor and his medical bag when making house calls.

Glossary, Makes of Cars

1. **Buick**: For years, Buicks were mid-priced to semi-luxury cars, built in Flint, Michigan. Buick was known for advanced motor design and in 1949 introduced the first "hardtop convertibles". Buick was founded by David Dunbar Buick who had previously invented the process for adhering porcelain to metal, making modern bathtubs we use today possible. Buick was the first auto company William C. Durant acquired to form General Motors Corporation.

2. **Graham**: Sometimes called Graham-Paige or Graham Brothers, the Graham was built in Dearborn, Michigan. A mid-priced car, with a flair for styling, some of its models were known for being quite fast.

3. **Mercury**: Just before World War II, the Ford Motor Co. began building the mid-priced Mercury to fill the gap between its low-priced Ford and its luxury car, the Lincoln. For a while, Mercurys were very popular.

4. **Packard**: The Packards were large luxury cars, sometimes having as many as twelve cylinders. At one time, more Packards were sold in America than all other luxury cars combined. Packards were built in Detroit, Michigan although for the first four years they were built in Warren, Ohio.

5. **Reo**: The Reos were well built mid-priced cars, made at Lansing, Michigan. Ransom E. Olds used his initials to name his new car, after he left Oldsmobile, which he'd founded a few years earlier.

6. **Studebaker**: The Studebaker Brothers Manufacturing Company had been in business for fifty years before it built its first car. Located in South Bend, Indiana, it was famous for its Conestoga covered wagons used by pioneers going west. Most Studebaker automobiles were low to mid-priced cars. Studebakers sometimes had unusually attractive or radically, unusual body styles.

7. **Willys**: Overlands and Willys Overlands were made in Toledo, Ohio. At first they were made in Terre Haute, and Indianapolis, Indiana. Most years there were two models, a mid-priced model, at one time called the Cardinal and the smaller economy model, like Willy, called the Bluebird. At one time, Willys Overlands were the second most sold car in America. Willys also made a more expensive car, the Willys-Knight and built the Willys Jeep.

EPILOGUE

The *Tale of Willy Willys* is based on the story of Willy Willys, a 1926 Willys Overland touring car. Since being found in terrible condition in a Minnesota pasture, Willy has been in parades, auto shows and brought great enjoyment to a host of riders. Today, when not entertaining riders, Willy stays in a secluded garage in Webster Groves, Missouri that has light yellow walls and a white and black tile floor. His current friends in the garage are a black 1912 International Harvester truck, a green and black 1919 Nash touring car, a red 1923 Dorris touring car, a yellow and black 1924 Moon touring car and a white 1956 Jaguar roadster.

Willy still starts right up when asked to because he's always ready for another joyful ride.